W9-BLP-711

+
E
G31ℓ

LOOK OUT, PATRICK!

Macmillan Publishing Company
866 Third Avenue, New York, NY 10022

First published in 1990 by
Hutchinson Children's Books, London, England

First American edition 1990
Printed and bound in Belgium

10 9 8 7 6 5 4 3 2 1

Designed by ACE Limited

Library of Congress Cataloging-in-Publication Data
Geraghty, Paul
    Look out, Patrick! Paul Geraghty
        p.   cm.
    Summary: Patrick the mouse goes for a pleasant walk,
oblivious to the many dangers that almost destroy him.
    ISBN 0-02-735822-4
[1. Mice – Fiction.] I. Title.
    PZ7.G29347Lo 1990 [E] – dc20 89-77850 CIP AC

LOOK OUT, PATRICK!

Paul Geraghty

Macmillan Publishing Company
New York

For Althea

Thanks to the Moppets for naming Patrick

One breezy afternoon Patrick was strolling home.

It was a lovely day, the birds were singing
and there was a spring in his step.
"The world is such a pleasant place," he said.

OH NO, PATRICK! LOOK OUT!

He gazed about in wonder.
The countryside was full of
delightful surprises:

the smell of new grass, the fresh green leaves and ripe red berries just ready to eat.

OH NO, PATRICK! LOOK OUT!

He bent down to sniff at a buttercup.

Bumblebees were buzzing back and forth busily. The air was sweet with the scent of nectar.

OH NO, PATRICK! LOOK OUT!

A butterfly tickled his whiskers,
and in the background water
gurgled. Patrick's tummy began
gurgling too.

wonder what's cooking in the
itchen, he thought.

H NO, PATRICK! LOOK OUT!

He tiptoed carefully. That nasty cat might be on the prowl.

There was no sign of the cat. But there *was* a nice big chunk of cheese.

"Mmmmm," said Patrick.
"My favorite snack."

OH NO, PATRICK! LOOK OUT!

Just then a delicious smell drifted by.
"Even better!" said Patrick.

"I wonder what it is."

OH NO, PATRICK! LOOK OUT!

He followed his nose as it
twitched and whiffed and
pointed and sniffed.
But suddenly . . .

OH NO, PATRICK! LOOK OUT!

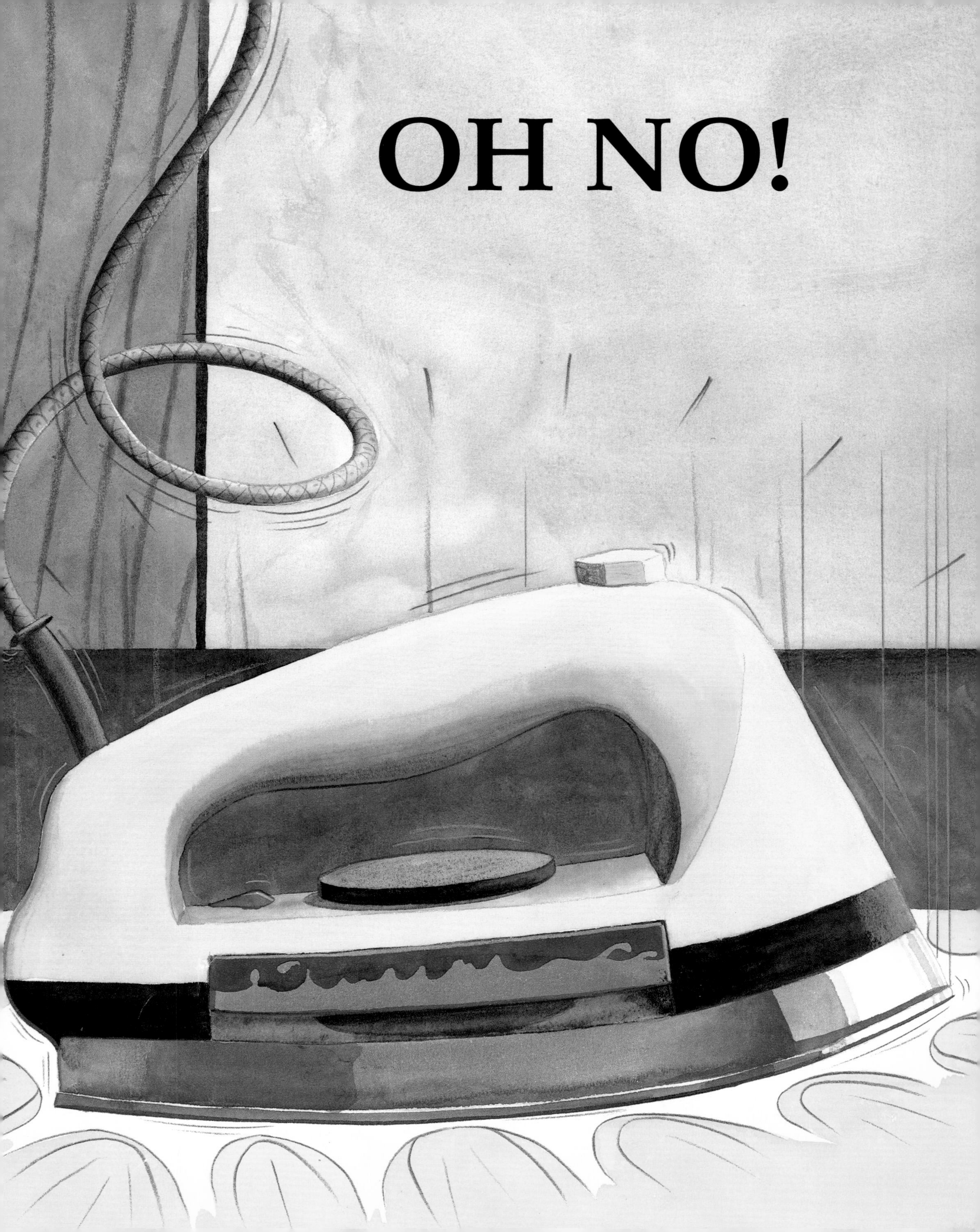

OH NO!

"That was a close one!
Must be my lucky day!"